THE SQUID

Tim Collins

Illustrated by James Lawrence

Titles in Monster Island:

THE APE
TIM COLLINS & ABBY RYDER

THE DINOSAUR
TIM COLLINS & JAMES LAWRENCE

THE SQUID
TIM COLLINS & JAMES LAWRENCE

THE YETI
TIM COLLINS & ABBY RYDER

THE CRAB
TIM COLLINS & JAMES LAWRENCE

THE CYCLOPS
TIM COLLINS & ABBY RYDER

Badger Publishing Limited, Oldmedow Road,
Hardwick Industrial Estate, King's Lynn PE30 4JJ

Telephone: 01438 791037
www.badgerlearning.co.uk

The Squid ISBN 978-1-78837-347-0

2 4 6 8 10 9 7 5 3 1

Publisher / Senior Editor: Danny Pearson
Editor: Claire Morgan
Series Consultant: Dee Reid
Designer: Fiona Grant
Cover Illustration: Mark Penman
Illustration: James Lawrence

Tim Collins

Illustrated by James Lawrence

Contents

Chapter 1	The Raft	6
Chapter 2	Attack	15
Chapter 3	Escape	23
Questions		31
Meet the Author and Illustrator		32

Story Vocabulary
paddle
tentacles
breath

The story so far…

Kyle was stuck on the island.

He had built a raft to escape.

"Welcome to Monster Island," said a man.
"I am the Captain. You will never escape."

Kyle laughed. He thought the Captain
was mad.

"Why is it called Monster Island?"
asked Kyle.

"You will soon find out," said the Captain.

Chapter 1

The Raft

Kyle dragged his raft across the beach.

He had to get away from the island.

Then he heard someone laughing.

It was the Captain.

"You won't be safe on that raft," he said.

Kyle looked at the sea. There were no waves.

"It looks OK to me," said Kyle.

"You are making a big mistake," said the Captain.

Kyle dragged his raft into the sea.

Then Kyle climbed onto the raft.

He lay down and began to paddle with his hands.

At first there were no waves.

But then the raft began to bob up and down.

Maybe the Captain was right, thought Kyle. *Maybe the raft is not safe.*

Just then, Kyle felt something slimy touch his leg.

Chapter 2

Attack

Kyle stood up.

He could see a dark shape below the raft.

It was huge.

The dark shape below the raft was a monster squid.

The monster had eight arms with thick suckers.

It had two huge green eyes as big as frisbees.

But the most scary things were the two very long tentacles.

The squid shot out its arms and hit the raft.

The raft rocked from side to side.

Kyle nearly fell into the water.

The squid grabbed the front of the raft with one of its huge tentacles.

It was trying to tip Kyle off.

No way! thought Kyle. *I'm not going to die!*

He took a deep breath and jumped into the water.

Chapter 3

Escape

Kyle swam towards the beach.

I must get away, he thought.

Kyle could feel the monster squid getting closer and closer.

I must swim faster, thought Kyle.

But his arms and legs were getting tired.

Then the monster squid shot out one of its long arms.

It gripped Kyle's ankle.

Kyle felt a burning pain.

He couldn't swim any more.

The monster was dragging Kyle towards its sharp beak.

Then it was going to slice him into bits.

Kyle saw a stick floating on the sea.

He grabbed the stick.

Then he twisted round and stabbed the end of the stick into one of the monster squid's huge green eyes.

Yucky green jelly shot out.

The monster let go of Kyle's leg.

Kyle swam for his life.

As he got near to the beach, he looked back.

The monster was twisting in the water. It was in pain.

At last, Kyle got to the beach and he lay on the hot sand.

Someone came up to him.

Kyle looked up. It was the Captain.

"Ha! Ha! Ha!" said the Captain. "I did warn you."

Kyle had got away from the monster but he was still stuck on the island.

Ape Mountain ✕

Yeti Cave ✕

Crab Cove ✕

Dinosaur Pen ✕

✕ Cyclops Forest

Squid Sea

SQUID INK

Questions
Chapter 1
Who is laughing at Kyle? *(page 8)*

What does the Captain say about Kyle's plan? *(page 10)*

Chapter 2
Describe the monster. *(page 18)*

What does the monster try to do? *(page 21)*

Chapter 3
How does Kyle stop the monster? *(page 26)*

How do you think Kyle feels at the end of the story?

About the Author

Tim Collins has written over 70 books for children and adults.

He lives near Oxford and spends his time listening to rock music and playing Pokémon.

He went to a real desert island once, but he didn't see any monsters.

About the Illustrator

James Lawrence loves reading comic books.

He lives in Manchester and he spends his days drawing cool pictures.

He thinks he could be friends with the Captain.